For everyone who disagrees with me

BEACH LANE BOOKS
An imprint of Simon & Schuster Children's Publishing Division
1230 Avenue of the Americas, New York, New York 10020
Copyright © 2020 by Bethanie Deeney Murguia
All rights reserved, including the right of reproduction in whole or in part in any form.
BEACH LANE BOOKS is a trademark of Simon & Schuster, Inc.
For information about special discounts for bulk purchases, please contact Simon & Schuster
Special Sales at 1-866-506-1949 or business@simonandschuster.com.
The Simon & Schuster Speakers Bureau can bring authors to your live event.
For more information or to book an event, contact the Simon & Schuster Speakers Bureau
at 1-866-248-3049 or visit our website at www.simonspeakers.com.
Book design by Rebecca Syracuse
The text for this book was hand-lettered.
The illustrations for this book were rendered with india ink, poster paints,
and block printing and were finished digitally.
Manufactured in China
0620 SCP
First Edition
10 9 8 7 6 5 4 3 2 1
CIP data for this book is available from the Library of Congress.
ISBN 978-1-5344-3880-4
ISBN 978-1-5344-3881-1 (ebook)

# WE DISAGREE

## Bethanie Deeney Murguia

**Beach Lane Books**
New York   London   Toronto   Sydney   New Delhi

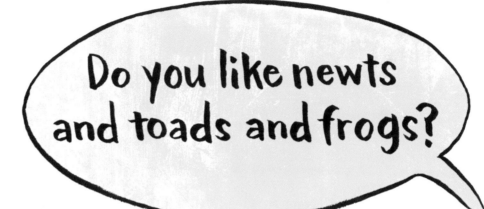

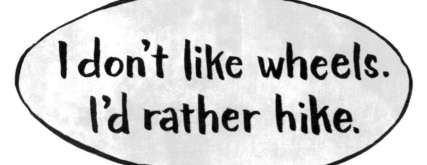

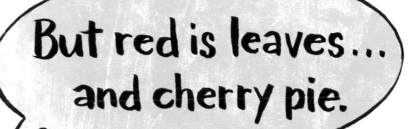